SILENT NIGHT

WILL MOSES
SILENT NIGHT

PHILOMEL BOOKS • NEW YORK

SILENT NIGHT

Once on a silent night in a place where snow clouds clung to the Vermont hills and lay heavily over every farmhouse and barn, over shops and country lanes, everyone was getting ready.

Benjamin Rogers, proprietor of the general store, was refilling his flour

barrels and stocking shelves. The carolers, including Teasy Simpson and little Ephraim Simpson, were gathering up their warmest scarves and toboggans, preparing to meet in the center of the town commons later that evening. Deacon Henry Heinz, from down by Parsons Creek, was already lighting the church lamps.

And up the valley somewhere beyond the Millers' farm, where the

headwaters of the Black Creek rise, Tom Henry and his little brother, Andy, were skating home with the evergreen they'd just cut in tow. On an ordinary day those two boys would frolic for hours on the ice, skating whirls and twirls, having the grandest time cutting fancy sixes and eights.

Today, though, was no ordinary day. The tree they were pulling was more gangly and unruly than they'd ever imagined when earlier they'd spied it growing in the nearby woods. And both boys knew this day might have more surprises left in it. So with all their might, they made a straight dash for home.

Tom Henry and Andy had to get ready, too.

HOLY NIGHT

Now look at that sky," James Miller called when he saw his boys coming across the field. "Beautiful. Just beautiful." He marched his milk cows right through a flock of hens that had been contentedly pecking about the farmyard, and off they shot, flapping and cackling like they'd been insulted. "It's a holy-night sky, boys. You'll want to remember this night."

It was indeed a beautiful early-evening sky, with brilliant splinters of fading pink sunlight still mingling wildly with blue and gray storm clouds on the distant horizon. "Oh, come on, boys, come on, then," James Miller said as the last cow was herded into the barn. "Let's see if we can't get to the station and back home again before the weather becomes unfit for man or beast. There's a train we've got to meet."

The boys knew Pa was talking about the 5:15 local from Bellows Falls.

"To pick up Grandma Stokes, Pa?" Tom Henry called out. "Well, Tom Henry," Pa called back, "don't she come every year, like clockwork?" He liked Grandma Stokes—General Grant, he called her when she was out of earshot.

Tom Henry and Andy finished up their chores—collecting eggs from the henhouse—all the while thinking how Pa had a lot more on his mind tonight than a snowstorm or the arrival of Grandma Stokes.

From the horse barn, Pa led old Peg and Mary, his favorite team, and hitched them to the sleigh. Tom Henry ran the basket of fresh eggs up to the house, fetched the warming stones for the sleigh, and he hung up his skates in the woodshed. Andy threw his skates over his shoulder and helped Pa with the team, for in the winter months, wherever Andy went, his skates went, too. Even to the train station.

ALL IS CALM

Then they all climbed into the sleigh and pulled up the buffalo robe. As they drove by the house, Pa took a last long look through the window of the room where Mama was. Then he barked, "Giddy-yap, Peg. Giddy-yap, Mary," and *whissh,* away they went, trotting down the snowy lane.

Andy knew Pa didn't want to leave home at all tonight. Not now, anyway.

Like a sheetful of cotton thrown to the wind, the snowflakes started falling before Peg and Mary had taken the sleigh a half mile down the lane. Past the sycamore and maple and oak trees, and between the stone walls that lined the old roadway, they trotted on. Through the covered bridge, the horses' hooves clopped over the rattly boards.

And then the sleigh glided out: it was suddenly quiet, like coming out of a dark, echoing cave into a white, feathery world again. Even the dull beat of the horses' hooves seemed distant now.

Andy pulled the buffalo robe up tighter. Usually when they made this trip, Pa would stop the sleigh and let him out just so he could skate the frozen river. He'd race down the icy stream, trying with all his might to beat Pa and his sleigh to Butternut Bend, where the river and road went their separate ways. Most times Andy would win. How that boy loved to skate.

Tonight, though, wasn't usually. Tonight, he just listened to the quiet of that snowy valley, a special quiet that seemed to surround them all.

"It won't be long now, boys," Pa said as the sleigh drove into town. Andy knew Pa was talking about more than catching the 5:15 train.

ALL IS BRIGHT

The little village was all astir as the townsfolk scurried about, doing last-minute errands. Light glowed from lantern upon lantern, and the windows twinkled, giving the shops and houses a magical appearance.

"Are you ready up at your place, then, James?" Fred, the blacksmith, called out as the sleigh passed. Fred was twisting up a fancy metal ornament in the brilliant orange fire of the forge —a special gift for his own dear wife.

Pa nodded and smiled through the feathery snow. "Yes, sir, Fred, nearly ready. Least my stocking is hung."

Fred just grinned and waved back.

As the sleigh went by the church, carolers began pouring out of the door, each bundled head to toe in woolens. And each with a lantern in one hand and a songbook in the other.

"My heavens, James, is this a time for you three boys to be out having a joyride for yourselves?" Teasy Simpson, the town's busybody, called out as she lit her own lantern.

"Meeting the five-fifteen," Pa called back. "Important visitor arriving, surprised you didn't know all about it."

Pa pulled the sleigh up to the general store, and went in just long enough to get some fresh coffee beans for General Grant—Pa knew Grandma liked her coffee strong and black. And while he was at it, he picked up some horehound candy from the barrel for himself and the boys. In case there was a wait at the station.

"A-yeh, James. Surprised to see you here today," Benjamin Rogers said, teasing Pa in his shopkeeper way. The other men, clustered around the potbellied stove just as they were every day, nodded. They, too, were prodding Pa to give up some gossip. Pa just popped a horehound candy into his mouth, smiled, and out of the store he walked.

Under way again, Andy could hear the distant moan of the train whistle as the team trotted past the town green, now white under its winter blanket. Past Foster's Wagon Shop, with its upper floor hanging over the road, back toward the river and Peterson's Grist Mill, its giant wheel still churning, over the bridge spanning the gorge with its gold-green water racing toward the Connecticut, Peg and Mary flew to meet the 5:15.

ROUND YON VIRGIN

It was Tinker, Mama's old quilty friend, who ran out of Mama's room and told Cozy, the milkmaid, who in turn ran to get Old Paul, the hired man,

who went down to the barn and rousted Josiah, the mule, out of his stall. He simply jumped on his bare back, and rode Josiah for all he was worth through that snowy night.

Surely Old Paul was worried about the weather, and he kept a wary eye on the cloud-puffed sky. Surely he was worried about James and the boys. But all said and done, Old Paul had bigger worries. Worries that drove him out into the stormy winter's night.

Old Paul was riding feverishly up Maiden Lane toward the big, crooked maple tree, when Doc Herrick saw him through his window. As wise as he was, Doc Herrick knew exactly why Old Paul was there. He gave a tender good-bye kiss to his sweet wife, Missy Herrick, and pulled on his boots, his overcoat, his hat,

and the striped muffler Missy had made for him that very December. Then, grabbing his bag, he gave the twins, Sophie and Olivia (who were not at all happy he was leaving), a hug and kiss, and he ran out to the barn.

Old Paul had already hitched Herrick's horse Jenny to the sleigh. Like a lightning bolt, the sleigh burst out of the barn doors into the deepening snow.

Luckily at the station the 5:15 was on time despite the storm, and naturally General Grant was the first off the train.

"There she is, just like I knew she would be," Pa said with a grin, and

with Grandma up front, they all climbed into the sleigh, squeezed tight among her satchels and sweet-smelling bundles. Doc Herrick and Old Paul, Pa and The General, Tom Henry and Andy were all going to the same place—the farm on Sycamore Lane.

"Do you think we will make it in time, James?" The General asked Pa. Her satchel nudged him in the ribs.

"We'll make it, Granny," Pa said. "It's Christmas Eve, isn't it?"

"I hope you're right," she said. A gust of icy wind stole her words. They all knew this would be a Christmas Eve like no other, and they went on into the dark, snowy night.

MOTHER AND CHILD

Doc Herrick got to the old farmhouse on Sycamore Lane first, and in minutes the place came alive. Old Paul had already finished stabling Jenny and was just crossing the farmyard when Pa's sleigh pulled up.

"Is it time?" Pa shouted to Old Paul.

"No, sir," said Paul. "Things are just starting to happen."

And sure enough, wasn't Old Paul right? No sooner had he walked into the house carrying a giant armful of wood for the cookstove than General Grant began to issue orders.

"Doc Herrick needs hot water! Paul, pump some, quick. Get it on the stove to boil. And Tinker, don't be in a hurry to leave on such a night

as this. You can help—start by making strong coffee. Like as not, we will want plenty of it." Then Cozy, the milkmaid, came in from doing chores. "Cozy," Grandma said, "we're going to need a meal before this night is out. See what you can find to put on the table to feed all these hungry folks!"

Pa's eyes twinkled as he grinned. With General Grant in charge, things were certainly bound to happen. Pa and everyone else there hoped it would be soon.

The tall old clock in the parlor, the one Andy liked so much, with the little moon creeping across the face, struck nine and then ten and then eleven o'clock. Pa, Tom Henry, and Andy had just enough time to trim the tree.

They had nearly forgotten about it. Grandma remembered, though, and made sure they got it up and in just the right spot!

They trimmed every branch of that tree, stringing it with popcorn and strands of fragrant apple curls and cranberries. They hung tin icicles and ornaments from the boughs, along with wonderful old glass balls, candy canes, and even some tiny rag dolls.

Then they set the tree candles and Pa lifted Andy up high so he could place the old glass star, the one that had been Mama's when she was a little girl, atop the tree. It was a crookedy old tree, and maybe they hadn't trimmed it just the way Mama would have done, but it was pert and

sparkly. Particularly with the glass star on top reflecting the light of the room the way it did. It shone sweetly and cast wonderful star shadows across the room.

"It's a miracle," said Pa. Andy knew Pa was talking about more than that twinkling glass star.

It was now nearly midnight. *Bong, bong, bong . . .* went the clock. Its sleepy little moon moved across its face until the clock struck twelve.

Well, it wasn't more than a minute or two after the clock clapped twelve when a cry went up in Mama's bedroom. It was a new voice. A new cry. Andy suddenly felt his heart lurch.

HOLY INFANT

Pa went in first with Tom Henry and little Andy. Didn't they creep in nice and quiet. Doc Herrick, certainly the wise one this night, was there, and so were Tinker and Cozy. Looking over everyone, of course, was The General. And there in bed, midst all these people, were Mama and a just-born, tiny little Christmas baby.

Somewhere out in the valley, carolers were singing. Maybe down at Sissy Atkins' or at the Jones Farm. Maybe they were singing their hearts out for the midnight service. Who knew? In that room, though, the only music heard—trumpets and angels' voices—came from some warm place inside each person, as everyone looked at Mama and her newborn baby for the first time.

"Now," whispered Pa, breaking the spell, "isn't that a holy child." Andy thought she was.

SO TENDER AND MILD

What started the gift-giving is hard to figure, it being so late and all. Tinker took a quilt she'd made by hand—it had sailboats, bears, and rocking horses, and all sorts of fine stitching. "Just right for the new baby," she said,

and tucked it up under the little baby's chin. Old Paul brought out a handsome, carved wooden horse. "Made from the old beech tree struck by lightnin' two years ago," he said with a smile. Cozy, not quite so handy with needle and thread, did in fact make a tiny little nightgown for the baby (out of a pretty old petticoat). With a blushing smile, she laid it out on the bed.

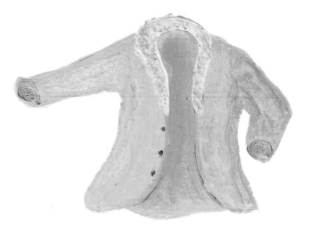

Granny rummaged around in one
of her bundles and soon enough
fished out a dandy little yellow
knit sweater with a hand-crocheted
lace collar. Right then she didn't seem
so much like General Grant after all.

Then Tom Henry stepped up to that baby, who seemed no bigger than

one of Pa's hands, and he gave her
the jar with the old bees' nest in
it—the one he found hanging in
the attic last spring. In the dim
twinkling light of that room, it
looked like a jar of jewels. Ma smiled

at Tom Henry, then back at the baby, so tender, so mild.

Little Andy wished he had known people were going to be giving gifts.

SLEEP IN HEAVENLY PEACE

Now the news went out over that snowy Vermont valley. Old Paul and Cozy saw to that. Down Sycamore Lane with its giant trees looking like white-haired, bearded kings. To the Atkins' farm, where the Atkins had just hung their stockings and gone to bed. Over to the Ketcham cottage, where they were trying their best not to open their gifts till morning. Just like the wintery north wind, the news of that night swept down the valley. Before long it even reached the carolers, who were just on their way home from singing at the midnight church service.

Well, didn't those wonderful, bone-tired carolers come trudging up Sycamore Lane when they heard the news? They formed up their choir right outside Mama's window, where that dear baby had just fallen asleep.

"Silent night, holy night," they sang, tenor voices rolling right into the dark. "Holy infant so tender and mild," they sang, the sopranos and altos harmonizing. "Sleep in heavenly peace," they sang all together. All those tired-but-loving voices, never sounding sweeter, sang out through the wintery night to that tiny little Christmas baby cradled in her mother's arms.

SLEEP IN HEAVENLY PEACE

Surely, it was a miracle. But now it was time for everyone to get some rest, at least that's what The General said. The carolers went home pretty quick after their last song, for the night was growing colder. They all had icy frost hanging from scarves and mustaches.

Tinker left with them, arm in arm, huddling close to keep warm. Old Paul went to his room over the woodshed; the ride and excitement sure had tuckered him out. Cozy crawled into bed in the little room off the kitchen and pulled three quilts snug, right up to her nose.

Doc Herrick and Jenny drove on home through the snow, though he knew well enough that the twins and Missy were fast asleep in their beds. He had missed Christmas Eve with them, but being part of a Christmas miracle was pretty special, too. Each time Doc brought a babe into this world, it seemed a miracle to him.

Pa took the candle, and he and Tom Henry slowly climbed up the stairs, singing in a loud whisper as they went, "Hark! the her-ald an-gels sing, Glory to the newborn King!" Pa turned when he saw Andy wasn't with them. "Come on along to bed, Andy, it's late."

But Andy didn't come. Instead, he went back to Mama's bedroom. Mama was sound asleep, and so was the babe. He quietly tiptoed over to the old featherbed.

And there he carefully laid down his precious skates.

"They are too big for you now, baby," he whispered, "but they're a promise. Someday, I'll teach you to skate just like me and Tom Henry. We'll make the fanciest sixes and eights that have ever been seen in this valley."

Now, as children often do, Andy crawled up onto that giant quilt-covered featherbed, lying so close to the baby that he could smell her baby sweetness. And it was right there that Andy fell asleep on that special night. A silent night, when a new baby came to a wintery Vermont valley, where snow clouds hung puffy over the hills and farms, barns, narrow lanes, and skating ponds.

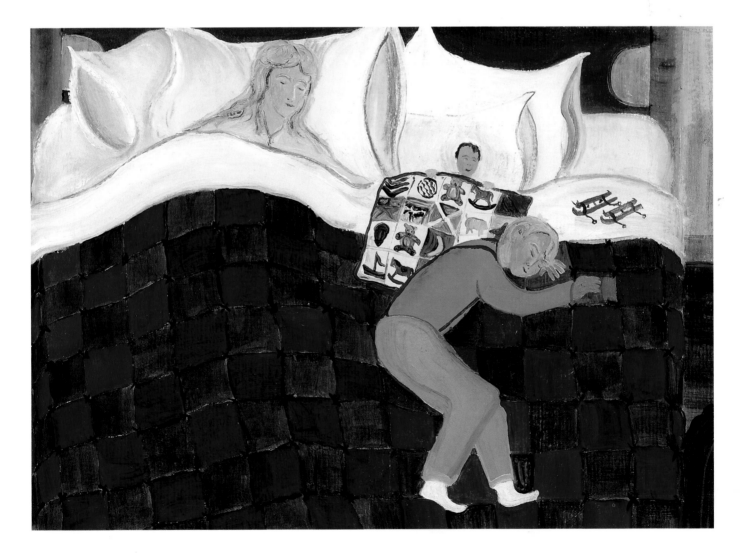

Only now, as Andy closed his eyes
for the night, the stars shone brightly.

SILENT NIGHT, HOLY NIGHT

Silent night, holy night!
All is calm, all is bright,
Round yon virgin mother and child!
Holy Infant, so tender and mild,
Sleep in heavenly peace,
Sleep in heavenly peace.

Silent night, holy night!
Shepherds quake at the sight,
Glories stream from heaven afar,
Heavenly hosts sing: "Alleluia;
Christ the Savior is born,
Christ the Savior is born."

Silent night, holy night!

Son of God, love's pure light

Radiant beams from Thy holy face,

With the dawn of redeeming grace,

Jesus, Lord, at Thy birth,

Jesus, Lord, at Thy birth.

Silent night, holy night!

Wondrous star, lend thy light;

With the angels let us sing,

Alleluia to our King;

Christ the Savior is born,

Christ the Savior is born.

For Georgianna Mary Moses

"Silent Night" was composed on Christmas Eve by Father Joseph Mohr and Franz Gruber in 1818.

Patricia Lee Gauch, Editor

Philomel Books, a division of The Putnam & Grosset Group, 200 Madison Avenue, New York, NY 10016.
Philomel Books, Reg. U.S. Pat. & Tm. Off. Published simultaneously in Canada.
Printed in Hong Kong by South China Printing Co. (1988) Ltd.
Book design by Gunta Alexander. The text is set in Garth Graphic.
Library of Congress Cataloging-in-Publication Data
Moses, Will. Silent night / written and illustrated by Will Moses. p. cm
Summary: One snowy Christmas Eve a Vermont community makes preparations for the holiday as well as
for the arrival of another Christmas miracle. [1. Christmas—Fiction. 2. Babies—Fiction.]
I. Title. PZ7.M8477Si 1997[Fic]—dc20 96-18585 CIP AC ISBN 0-399-23100-5 (hardcover)
3 5 7 9 10 8 6 4 2